MAXIMILIAN P. MOUSE, TIME TRAVELER

HOMEWARD BOUND

CIVIL RIGHTS MOUSE LEADER

magic
wagon

BOOK 6

Philip M. Horender • Guy Wolek

visit us at www.abdopublishing.com

To my family past and present, for helping make me who I am today—PMH

Published by Magic Wagon, a division of the ABDO Group, PO Box 398166, Minneapolis, Minnesota 55439. Copyright © 2014 by Abdo Consulting Group, Inc. International copyrights reserved in all countries. All rights reserved. No part of this book may be reproduced in any form without written permission from the publisher.

Calico Chapter Books™ is a trademark and logo of Magic Wagon.

Printed in the United States of America, North Mankato, Minnesota.
052013
092013

Text by Philip M. Horender
Illustrations by Guy Wolek
Edited by Stephanie Hedlund and Rochelle Baltzer
Cover and interior design by Neil Klinepier

Library of Congress Cataloging-in-Publication Data
Horender, Philip M.
  Homeward bound : civil rights mouse leader / by Philip M. Horender ; illustrated by Guy Wolek.
      p. cm. -- (Maximilian P. Mouse, time traveler ; bk. 6)
  Summary: Maximilian arrives at the Lincoln Memorial in 1963, in time to observe Dr. Martin Luther King Jr.'s "I have a dream speech" and then finally makes it home on the original target date but still must figure out a way to save Farmer Tanner's farm.
  ISBN 978-1-61641-962-2
1. King, Martin Luther, Jr., 1929-1968. I have a dream--Juvenile fiction.
2. Mice--Juvenile fiction. 3. Time travel--Juvenile fiction. 4. Washington (D.C.)--History--20th century--Juvenile literature. [1. King, Martin Luther, Jr., 1929-1968. I have a dream--Fiction. 2. Mice--Fiction. 3. Time travel--Fiction. 4. Adventure and adventurers--Fiction. 5. Washington (D.C.)--History--20th century--Fiction.] I. Wolek, Guy, ill. II. Title.
  PZ7.H78087Hom 2013
  813.6--dc23
                            2012050866

TABLE OF
CONTENTS

Chapter 1: A Strange Place 4
Chapter 2: Washington, DC 7
Chapter 3: A Stranger 12
Chapter 4: Marian Moleana 15
Chapter 5: 100 Years Old 19
Chapter 6: Where Were We? 24
Chapter 7: A Loophole 29
Chapter 8: Gaining Momentum 35
Chapter 9: The Gathering Place 40
Chapter 10: Free At Last! 48
Chapter 11: A New Souvenir 54
Chapter 12: Learn to See 61
Chapter 13: A Familiar Place 64
Chapter 14: Home 68
Chapter 15: Finally! 71
Chapter 16: The Bad News 75
Chapter 17: Aha! 79
Chapter 18: An Idea Forms 83
Chapter 19: Waiting for Nightfall 87
Chapter 20: It's Time 90
Chapter 21: Mission Accomplished 94
Chapter 22: Time to Go Home 99
Chapter 23: Another Try 102
About the Civil Rights Movement 106
Glossary 108
About the Author 112

Chapter 1:
A STRANGE PLACE

Maximilian's body ached as he removed the seat belt and stretched. He breathed a heavy sigh of relief that Nathaniel's invention had survived the slight crack to its shell and that he was okay.

Maximilian pulled out his handkerchief and unlatched the portal lock. The door swung open and he climbed out.

"Please," Maximilian said to himself. "Please let me be in Tanner's Glen."

Maximilian jumped to the ground and immediately felt a sense of dread. His paws landed on smooth, polished marble. The marble felt cool on the pads of his feet. He stood in the shadow of something large, the time machine cooling behind him.

Maximilian rubbed his eyes and stared at the ground. Not only was the ground made of marble, but the walls around him seemed to be as well.

Maximilian skirted the marble base, careful to keep his back close to the wall. He left the shadows and walked into soft moonlight. He saw several amazingly tall pillars at the mouth of the building he was in.

This building, this architecture, did not look like anything he had ever seen before.

The pillars towered over him. They were definitely nowhere near the height of the Statue of Liberty. But they were taller than any of the trees in his forest back home. Unfortunately though, these were not trees, and this was not his forest.

Maximilian slowly turned to see what the marble base supported. His jaw dropped. His eyes could not comprehend what they saw.

Maximilian's paw went to his open mouth. Before him was a gigantic statue of a man seated in a chair. This grand theater housed a statue in honor of President Abraham Lincoln.

Chapter 2

WASHINGTON, DC

Maximilian sat on the stone steps at the front of the monument. It was night out, wherever he was. The sky was clear and black and the moonlight sliced like a knife through the empty darkness.

The small field mouse leaned back on his paws and looked out over the landscape. The line of the horizon blurred. It was difficult to determine where the stars stopped and the lights of the city skyline began.

The night was warm. Maximilian patted dust from his vest. He began to calculate all the different places and time periods he had already visited to this point.

He had started in Boston, on the eve of the American Revolution in 1773. Then he had found himself in **rural** Gettysburg, Pennsylvania, for President Lincoln's famous speech during the Civil War. The year had been 1863. Maximilian glanced back at his old friend, who sat in marble behind him.

After Gettysburg, Maximilian had traveled with the Franklin family to Silver Springs and Promontory Point, Utah. There, he watched the historic driving of the Golden Spike, completing the **transcontinental** railroad. The spike had been driven in 1869.

Maximilian shook his head in disbelief. All of these memories, these adventures, ran like a filmstrip through his mind. He was glad he had kept such detailed descriptions of each stop in his journal. He wanted to remember everyone he had met.

From Utah, Maximilian had found himself next on the muddy waters of the Mississippi River. He rode aboard the pristine *Mississippi Belle*. The year was 1875. Maximilian had spent Christmas with his merry friends, Bogart T. Bullfrog and Samuel Clemens.

It was important for Maximilian to remind himself of his original goal—to save Tanner's Glen and his family's home.

From the banks of the Southern bayou, Maximilian had traveled to New York Harbor. Along with Irish **immigrants**, Maximilian had entered the bay with hope.

Hope. It was all he had left at this point.

The lights to the monument housing President Lincoln shone brightly at his back.

Where was he now? What year was it? Had the time machine brought him any closer to finding his way home?

A young couple strode past him. They laughed. The woman was dressed in a flowing white skirt. She had her arm draped through a man's arm. The man was tall and walked with long, easy strides. His hand was placed affectionately on top of the girl's. They passed by Maximilian, completely unaware of his presence. The sound of their steps on the hard marble slabs echoed in the air.

Maximilian noticed that the couple passed by a community bulletin board. He began slowly climbing down the steps. There seemed to be hundreds of them. It took him some time, partly because of his size, but also because he was tired.

Finally, Maximilian reached the bottom of the mountain of marble steps. He used what remaining energy he had to run to the outdoor bulletin board. It was cluttered with dozens of announcements, flyers for rallies, and notices of future gatherings. They were layered on top of one another, pinned to the board with tacks and tape.

Many of the posters were old. Others were torn and ruined from rain and wind. Maximilian scanned them for clues as to where he was and what date the time machine had stopped in.

One poster stood out from the rest. It had been placed carefully in the very center of the bulletin board, all four sides fastened down securely. Maximilian's gaze fell directly on it:

March on Washington for Jobs and Freedom

"Washington," Maximilian said.   He remembered Washington being mentioned at several points along his journey.

It was quiet in Washington this night. Maximilian removed his pocket watch. It was three o'clock in the morning.

Maximilian continued reading the poster:

Help Shed Light on the Political and Social Challenges Facing Our Country Today.   Organized By the National Association for the Advancement of Colored People and the Southern Christian Leadership Conference.

Maximilian ran a paw through the fur that stood stiffly on top of his head. His eyes fell on the last line of this poster:

Rally to Be Held on the Steps of the Lincoln Memorial August 28, 1963.

Chapter 3:
A STRANGER

The time machine had gotten the location wrong six times now. But, each jump in time had brought Maximilian closer to 2013. In this case, he had managed to fast-forward nineteen years.

Closer, but still a long ways off, Maximilian thought. He decided to return to the time machine and figure out what he was up against. Maximilian was not sure how much more luck he would have on this journey.

Maximilian delayed the climb back up the stairs by looking around the Lincoln Memorial. In the darkness, he had not really been able to fully appreciate Washington.

The Lincoln Memorial stood at the head of a long, rectangular pool. Maximilian could only guess how long the man-made body of water was, but it was impressive.

In the quiet morning hours, the water stood clear and still. Maximilian looked deep and hard at the reflection in the water. His clothes were dirty and wrinkled. His hair was a mess. Maximilian reached out toward his reflection. His soft, gray finger broke the surface of the water and his image changed. Maximilian sighed.

At the other end of the long pool was another structure. It was a tall, slender **obelisk** surrounded by American flags.

That, he thought, *may be just as tall as the Statue of Liberty!*

Maximilian turned and looked up at the stairs that lay before him.

"Well," he said to himself, "get busy standing or get busy climbing." Maximilian began his climb. He was able to jump up one step to the next. Pausing briefly between steps to catch his breath and rest his legs, Maximilian slowly made his way upward.

The inside of the memorial was huge. At the moment, it was empty and quiet. Maximilian was alone with his own heavy breathing.

Maximilian tried to imagine what it would be like in the morning. He pictured this monument full of tourists.

Maximilian wondered just how safe the time machine was. He had never tried to move it in the past. He doubted he could. Besides, he wasn't willing to risk another accident that might damage the acorn shell.

Maximilian rounded the **pedestal** where Lincoln sat. He tried to decide which was more important, sleep or finding food. The early morning hours provided the best time for a mouse to hunt and Maximilian was hungry.

Turning the corner, the time machine came into view. He froze and held his breath. There, at the side of the time machine, stood another animal. Its back was to Maximilian, and it was running its paw over the smooth, polished exterior.

Chapter 4:
MARIAN MOLEANA

Before Maximilian could think of what to say, the animal turned to face him. It was a mole, whose coat had long ago turned gray. Her back was hunched like a question mark, and she depended on a walking stick to support her weight. Maximilian noticed something else peculiar about her. Despite wearing glasses, her eyes were almost completely shut.

"Did your mother ever tell you that it was rude not to introduce yourself to someone you just met?" the elderly mole said in a stern tone.

Maximilian did not say anything. He should have though. She was right. He was indeed being very **impolite**.

The truth was, Maximilian was still trying to determine how she had known he was there!

His soft, padded feet had not made a sound on the smooth, even marble.

"Mmm, mmm . . . ," she said again in disgust. "I simply do not understand how animals are being raised these days." Tapping her stick on the ground with a loud clicking sound, she started a very slow walk in his direction.

"My apologies," Maximilian managed to stammer. "My name is Maximilian . . . Maximilian P. Mouse."

The mole stopped and turned an ear toward him. "A mouse, say you?" she said. "Well then, my boy, your apology is accepted. It is nice to make your **acquaintance**.

"The name is Marian Moleana," the mole said in a quieter, more sensitive tone. She immediately reminded Maximilian of his grandmother, which made him long to be home. He missed his family terribly.

Marian continued past Maximilian. She shuffled her feet and used her walking stick on the slick marble floor.

"Hungry, Maximilian?" she asked. She motioned for him to follow her.

"Yes, ma'am. I'm quite hungry," Maximilian admitted. "But, I certainly do not want to **impose**." His stomach made a low, painful groan as if on cue.

Marian stopped and chuckled.

"Sounds like your belly would object to that last remark," she said.

Maximilian rubbed his stomach in embarrassment.

"Well, I will not take no for an answer," Marian insisted. "I have a fresh loaf of pumpernickel bread just ready to be cut and buttered. I can smell it from here!"

Maximilian could hear the excitement in her voice. He wondered how many guests she received. He decided that saying no to her would be rude.

Besides, Maximilian thought, *I definitely have the time.*

"You know, Ms. Moleana," Maximilian spoke again, "I think I can smell that bread, too."

Marian nodded in agreement.

"Good, it's settled then," she said, quite pleased with herself. "And while we eat, you can tell me more about that **contraption** of yours behind Mr. Lincoln's statue."

Chapter 5:
100 YEARS OLD

The statue in the Lincoln Memorial was completed in 1920 by the artist David Chester French. Maximilian read the small plaque fastened to the back wall of the memorial. The plaque was approximately two inches off the ground. It had been molded in bronze, the script simple and worn.

Maximilian watched as Marian counted to herself under her breath. She made her way toward the plaque. Then, she wet her fingers and began to unscrew the top left-hand corner.

Marian did not speak as she worked. In a few seconds, the screw had been loosened enough that the sign swung to the side. A hole appeared that was just large enough for Marian to climb through.

It was not until she was fully inside that Maximilian heard her call back to him.

"Are you coming or are you staying, Mr. Maximilian?" Marian called.

Maximilian shrugged. He had managed to get himself into some rather peculiar situations on his trip. The time machine appeared to be safely hidden in the shadow of the Lincoln statue. Maximilian climbed inside. He was careful to make sure his tail was securely behind him before he replaced the plaque.

It was so dark inside the hole that Maximilian had a difficult time determining which direction to go. He reminded himself that Marian was indifferent to the darkness.

"Hello," Maximilian called out. He heard nothing and received no response.

"Just a moment," Marian finally echoed back to him.

Maximilian strained to hear rustling far off in the tunnel. Finally, he heard a sound like the striking of a match. Suddenly, the entire tunnel was lit. Maximilian could now see it was only a few feet long.

The walls of the tunnel were smooth and damp. Maximilian decided that the **burrow** was made of clay, similar to that found on the damp creek banks of Tanner's Glen.

Maximilian smelled warm bread in the near distance. His belly growled again, prodding him to move toward the candle.

Maximilian continued toward the light. He entered a small, narrow doorway. Inside, Marian stood at a counter in the corner and dried her hands on a linen washcloth.

"Is this your home?" Maximilian asked. He was not quite sure where to stand or if he should sit down.

"Yes, it is," Marian responded quickly, with a hint of pride in her voice. "I know it's not much, but it keeps me dry from the rain and warm from the cold. It fits me just fine."

"It's nice. I like it, Marian," Maximilian said, reassuring her. Maximilian found her home warm and welcoming.

"Please have a seat, Maximilian," Marian said. She waved her paw in the direction of an antique rocking chair in the center of the room. "That is, if you haven't sat down already," she joked.

Maximilian smiled and took a seat in the chair. Marian opened the door to a stove on the side of the sink. Maximilian did not know of any animals that had modern stoves in their kitchens. Many, like his mother, cooked over open wood pits or **hearths**.

"That is an impressive oven, Marian," Maximilian said. "How long have you lived here?" he asked.

Marian was carefully slicing the bread. She paused and thought for a moment. She shook her head as if she had figured out the answer to a mathematical equation.

"I moved to Washington, DC in the summer of 1920. It was the same year Mr. French was completing his masterpiece of Lincoln. The **architect** Henry Bacon was also finishing the Greek cathedral it's housed in," she said.

"The stove and the plumbing in the rear room were all gifts of my son, Leonard. He happens to be an architect as well," she finished.

Maximilian was impressed. "Well, all sons want their mothers to be safe and comfortable," he said. "He does some fine work."

"He worries about me, my poor Leonard," Marian said. She felt her way over a cutting board and grabbed a washcloth.

"I can appreciate that," Maximilian said. "I worry about my mother and my sister constantly."

Marian moved around the room with ease. She soon placed a warm slice of bread covered with cranberry jam in front of him.

"Leonard has worried about me living on my own since I lost my eyesight," Marian said. She positioned herself in a chair next to him with a small cup of tea. "There's that and the birthday I just celebrated this past week," she continued.

Maximilian finished chewing and cleared his throat. "Hmm, happy birthday, Marian! How old are you?" he said before he could catch himself. "I'm sorry, that was very rude of me. I shouldn't have asked."

Marian laughed and rocked back in her chair.

"Don't be silly, child," she said. "Why, I just turned 100 years old last Tuesday!"

Chapter 6:
WHERE WERE WE?

Maximilian stopped mid-bite and stared at Marian Moleana in disbelief. He did not know that animals of any kind could live that long—100 years!

"That's remarkable!" Maximilian exclaimed.

Marian laughed some more and slapped her knee.

"Why, yes, I suppose it is," Marian said in agreement. "I have led a very blessed life."

Maximilian thought of all the things Marian must have seen and experienced in her lifetime. It dawned on him that if it was indeed 1963, she had been born in 1863. That was the year of the Battle of Gettysburg.

"You were born the same year Lincoln gave his famous speech," Maximilian said. He couldn't wait to hear stories of what Marian had lived through.

"That is a very good **observation**, Maximilian," Marian said. She stopped to stare at him in amazement. "Did you notice that the entire Gettysburg Address is engraved on the eastern wall of the monument?" she asked.

Maximilian shook his head. He had not noticed much beyond the massive statue of the president he adored. The time he had spent with him in the Willses' house was still fresh in his mind.

Marian rocked gently in her chair and took a slight sip of her tea. Steam rose from the porcelain cup.

"I was born a month before that fateful turning point in our country's history," she said as if she were recalling an event from her own family's history.

"I don't remember exactly where I was born," Marian continued. "My family traveled a lot when I was a child. We visited places like Alabama, Arkansas, and Georgia."

Maximilian had traveled through many states during his quest, but those three had not made his list.

"Those were rough states during that time, you understand," Marian said matter-of-factly. "My parents did whatever they could to keep the family together and to help us survive."

The light in Marian's burrow burned low. Shadows grew long on the clay walls that surrounded them. It made for a rather **eerie**

setting as Maximilian listened to Marian talk about her childhood during the Civil War.

"We made it though," she said with a look of pride. "I guess you could say that my early years were not easy. But they made for a better future and helped shape who I am today."

Maximilian took another hearty bite of his bread. The pain in his stomach had subsided and he was beginning to feel at ease with Marian.

"What did your family do after the war?" Maximilian asked. He hoped Marian could fill in the gaps between one time machine journey to the next.

"Well, where do I begin?" she said shyly. Maximilian could see how much she enjoyed having a guest to listen to the stories she had compiled over 100 years on this earth.

"Let me get you another piece of bread before I begin," Marian said and got to her paws. Amazingly, Maximilian had not even noticed that his bread was nearly gone.

How had she known?

Since nearly bumping in to Marian at the Lincoln statue, she had surprised Maximilian. He was amazed at how much she could do despite being blind.

Marian returned from the kitchen with another piece of bread. She sat back down in her chair, its old legs creaking faintly. She crossed her paws in front of her and began to rock—slowly and rhythmically like the ticking of Maximilian's pocket watch.

"Now," Marian began in her soft voice, "where were we?"

Chapter 7:
A LOOPHOLE

Maximilian was full. He simply could not eat another bite and it felt good. He reflected on all of the amazing food he'd had on his journey and considered creating a cookbook, if and when he ever made it home.

"After the war, the South began a period called **Reconstruction**. They tried to rebuild and get themselves back on their paws," Marian explained. She continued to slowly rock.

"My father took our family wherever the work was," she said. "We helped animals rebuild homes that had been lost in battle. We helped repair the tunnel network that allowed others to go North after they had lost everything."

The candle that sat on the living room table burned low as Marian talked. Soon, wax collected in its holder and threatened to run over onto the table runner.

"My father was a great mole and a hard worker," Marian said, nodding. "He never complained and never made excuses. He did whatever he needed to in order to provide for my mother and me."

Maximilian's watch chimed and Marian's ears perked up. It was six o'clock.

"That is a glorious timepiece you have, Maximilian," she declared. "Now where did you get such a fine watch?"

Maximilian smiled and closed his eyes, placing his watch carefully back in his pocket.

"My father," he said. "I lost him when I was very young. I, quite honestly, don't remember anything about him. I envy you for having such fond memories of your father."

"That must be difficult, child," Marian said in her grandmother-like way. "He must have thought very highly of his son to leave such a fine **heirloom** to him. I just met you and I can already tell how proud he would be of the mouse you have become."

Maximilian hoped that was true.

"I loved my father, too," Marian said. "He passed away shortly after we moved to the state of Virginia. I was still fairly young and it was unexpected."

"I'm very sorry to hear that," Maximilian said, returning the support she had shown him.

"My mother died shortly after my father, about two years to the day," Marian continued. "She was never the same without him, truth be told."

Maximilian eyed a ball of yarn and a pair of needles resting in the corner. A partial throw blanket was draped nearby. He had wondered how she might pass the time.

"I was an only child. Practically overnight I was on my own," Marian said, taking a break for a sip of tea. She blew slightly on the cup before putting it to her lips.

"The next few years, I spent afraid of much of the world. I moved from one Southern woodland to the next," Marian said.

"I got to experience what the South was truly like in the years following the Civil War,"

Marian continued. "Now don't get me wrong, there were many good animals that helped me survive. But many were also bitter about the way the war had ended."

"Bitter?" Maximilian asked. He was reminded of the talks he had shared with Bogie on the decks of the *Mississippi Belle*. He thought about what Bogie had told him and decided to add something into the conversation.

"You mean that just because laws are passed in the nation's capital, doesn't mean that people are going to start changing the way they've thought for **generations**?" Maximilian said. "A friend of mine once told me that the fears and **prejudices** people in the South had helped contribute to the war. In some cases, they still showed themselves after the war."

Marian said nothing. She stopped rocking and placed her cup on the saucer on the table in front of her.

"You have some smart friends," Marian said. "Why, you sound pretty intelligent yourself." The candle flickered and threatened to go out entirely.

"States that had lost the Civil War," she explained, "found loopholes in laws that the government had passed. Do you know what 'loophole' means, Maximilian?"

Maximilian considered the question. It was definitely a word he had heard before, but its definition escaped him.

"No, I'm afraid I don't," he said.

"A loophole is a way to avoid following a law. Interestingly enough, it is the reason for what we will see today in front of the monument," the elderly mole explained to the young field mouse.

The candle went out, leaving the two new friends sitting together in the dark.

"The fact that the country did not unite and overcome its differences after the war is the reason rallies are held. It is the reason the one being held here this afternoon is necessary," Marian explained. She was talking about the poster from the bulletin board that Maximilian had read earlier.

So it was August 28, 1963.

"I saw the flyer for that gathering out in front of the memorial," Maximilian said. "It mentioned someone by the name of Dr. Martin Luther King Jr. being the keynote speaker."

Marian lit a second, partially melted candle.

"Ah, yes," she said. "I was about to tell you about that very gentlemen in my next story." She reached for her knitting and continued to work on her blanket.

"Dr. Martin Luther King Jr.," she said, "has tried to close that loophole in our country's history."

Chapter 8:
GAINING MOMENTUM

"When my father would look for work in the South after the Civil War, there were some animals that refused to hire him," Marian said. The blanket she was knitting began to snake its way onto the floor.

"It sounds as though he was a skilled craftsman," Maximilian said. "Why then would some animals not even hire him?"

The candle flickered. It was quiet in the mole's den, the only sound the clicking of knitting needles.

"It goes back to what we spoke about earlier," Marian explained, not missing a stitch as she talked. "Depending on what species of animal you happened to be, what state you were from, or how dark your fur was, many employers chose not even to hire you.

"The Civil War had managed to split this country at its seams," Marian said, taking a break from her knitting and rubbing her eyes. "In the process, it exposed some very dark things about the way some thought about those who are different from themselves."

Maximilian wrapped his tail around himself.

"You mentioned Dr. King has tried to bring people together, to end some of these prejudices," Maximilian said.

"Yes," Marian replied, nodding. "He's not a doctor in the traditional sense, but in the philosophical meaning."

Maximilian thought he understood. His history teacher was a doctor and had gone to the Academy of Birchwood. Dr. Marcellus S. Muskrat, was quite honestly the most brilliant speaker and scholar that Maximilian knew.

"Dr. Martin Luther King Jr. is from Atlanta, Georgia. He is also the pastor of his church," Marian said. "He's become the leader of the civil rights movement. He fights for African Americans and other **minorities** who still do not have the same rights as others living in the United States."

"Even after 100 years?" Maximilian asked wide-eyed. "Do minorities in this country still not have equal rights?"

Marian was back to knitting.

"No, my child," she said shamefully. "I'm afraid not. Dr. King is trying to change that and to mend the wounds of the Civil War once and for all. It's been said that time heals everything, but it has failed to in this case."

Marian continued by saying, "Dr. King has been able to bring this movement and people from all kinds of backgrounds together with a single focus." She paused and concentrated on her words. "He's young, **charismatic**, and hopeful . . . I think."

"Hopeful?" Maximilian echoed. There was that word again. It seemed to be a common theme in all of this. "In what sense?" he asked.

Marian stopped her knitting again. She

stopped rocking. She looked in Maximilian's direction and pursed her lips.

"He's been able to convince many people, and animals, that our differences are outweighed by our similarities," Marian said. It was a beautiful statement. She might be a simple mole, but her words struck him.

"The movement toward equal rights has been gaining **momentum** under his leadership," she continued. "There have been **boycotts** in Montgomery and marches in Memphis. I think that many are hopeful that today's message will bring it all together. They hope it will be the next big step toward achieving the movement's goal."

"What is the goal of the movement?" Maximilian asked.

"The goal, I think, is to finally make this a country—a home—that our beloved President Lincoln had wanted 100 years ago," Marian said. A sweet smile made its way across her kind face.

Maximilian smiled too. He was glad he had met Marian. Their conversation had built anticipation in him for the day's events, which included another trip in the time machine.

Chapter 9:
THE GATHERING PLACE

Without Maximilian's pocket watch it would have been impossible for him to tell exactly what time it was. He was too excited to be tired. He couldn't wait to witness another historic day in American history.

When it was time, Maximilian swung the metal plate hiding the tunnel to the side. When he saw it was safe to go out, he helped Marian through the small opening.

"Ever the young gentleman," she said, gleefully grasping his arm.

The afternoon at the nation's capital was cloudy and overcast. A large crowd had gathered in the mall that Maximilian had stood alone in hours earlier.

"Wow!" Maximilian exclaimed.

"How many?" Marian asked after hearing his reaction.

"I can't even begin to guess," Maximilian said. Marian smiled when she heard the awe in his voice. "I would have to say 50,000 people if not more, although it's difficult to see from where we are."

No sooner had the words left his mouth, than Maximilian heard a voice call out from above them.

"We were wondering when you were going to be joining us," a beige mole said through cupped paws. The mole was wearing a bow tie, a plaid vest, and an enormous smile. He peered down from on top of the Lincoln statue base.

"Leonard, you knew I would not miss this for anything," Marian said, returning the smile.

"That's your son?" Maximilian asked.

Marian nodded.

"I'm guessing he's with his wife, Judith Anne, and their two friends Earl and Elaine," Marian said to Maximilian.

Leonard vanished for a second and returned just as quickly.

"We'll lower the pail for you and your friend," he said in a loud and clear voice.

Marian leaned toward Maximilian as if to tell him a secret. "My son thinks that my hearing is as poor as my vision," she said playfully. Maximilian chuckled.

A small tin bucket tied to a white rope was slowly lowered in their direction. When it reached the marble floor, Maximilian helped Marian inside and then climbed in behind her. Although it was obviously nothing like the soaring flight he had taken with Captain Patton over New York Harbor, Maximilian felt butterflies form in the pit of his stomach.

"Hold on!" Leonard instructed and the pail lifted off the ground. It did not take long before they had been hoisted twenty to thirty feet in the air. Soon, they were sitting comfortably in the company of the other moles gathered for the day's festivities.

Marian introduced the young field mouse to her son, his wife, and the couple they were with. Judith Anne was similar in color to her husband, although slightly blonder, while Earl and Elaine were a darker shade of brown.

Earl wore a yellow necktie done up with a masterful Windsor knot and a velvet-lined hat. He touched the hat's brim in a friendly gesture to Maximilian. Judith Anne and Elaine wore plain dresses and fanned themselves with paper fans.

The **humidity** of the August day was clear in Maximilian's fur. It refused to lie down properly and stood at attention between his ears.

The sea of people between the Lincoln Memorial and the obelisk that Maximilian had seen the night before was simply stunning. People of all colors and ages had gathered. A **podium** now stood several feet in front of the memorial's columns.

"What have the boy and I missed so far?" Marian asked. She had taken a seat at the base of Lincoln's right shoe. She was digging through a small bag she had brought with her. Maximilian watched as she removed her knitting needles and the blanket she had been working on. He shook his head in wonder at what a **unique** character Ms. Marian Moleana was proving to be.

Judith Anne turned the page of a paw-written event program that each of the moles had. She stopped on the second sheet.

"Let's see," Judith Anne began, "we've already heard a number of speeches, prayers, and poetry from several different clergymen, authors, and politicians." The view from the Lincoln statue showed the joyous crowd that had gathered in the plaza that day.

"John Lewis of the Student Non-Violent Coordinating Committee just finished talking," Judith Anne continued. "He has been a very vocal **critic** of President John F. Kennedy," she said. "Someone must have told him ahead of time not to be too harsh on the president. His speech was tame."

Marian turned her head into the warm summer breeze. She continued to knit and listen to the other moles discuss the day's events.

Earl straightened his tie and turned his attention to Maximilian. He asked, "Are you familiar with Bob Dylan, my good man?"

It took Maximilian a moment to realize that the question was for him. "No, I'm afraid I'm not," he said. "Is he a politician?"

Earl smiled and shook his head.

"No, actually he's a very popular singer and **activist**," he said. "He just got done singing. I'm sorry you missed it." Earl looked at his wife, Elaine, who was glancing through the remainder of the program.

"He's next!" Elaine said excitedly. "Dr. Martin Luther King Jr. is scheduled to speak next!"

Maximilian and the moles talked amongst themselves upon hearing this news. The people gathered below did as well.

Police officers stood at attention on the edge of the crowd. Some wore dark sunglasses. Others had large dogs—German shepherds to be exact—on leashes. Maximilian was sure they were there to simply keep control over such a large group. But their presence was quite **intimidating**.

As the main stage remained empty and time went by, the crowd grew louder and more restless. Maximilian scanned the crowd and wondered which of them was Dr. King.

Suddenly, a hush fell over the crowd. No announcement had been made. No introduction was heard. Maximilian looked to the podium. An African-American man had stepped to the microphone. He was dressed in a plain black suit with a white shirt and a black tie.

Much to Maximilian's amazement, he was not a towering figure. If this man had been amongst them, it would have been nearly impossible to pick him out from the crowd. But he had just now silenced tens of thousands of people by standing at a podium.

The moles sat quiet. Those gathered on the lawn of the most powerful **democracy** in the world stood silent as well.

Dr. Martin Luther King Jr. was ready to speak.

Chapter 10:
FREE AT LAST!

The somewhat dreary, overcast day gave way to rays of sunshine. Maximilian sat with Marian and the other moles, **riveted** to the man who had just taken the podium.

And then, Dr. King began to address the crowd.

Dr. Martin Luther King Jr. delivered a speech unlike anything Maximilian had ever witnessed before. This man began his speech as more of a preacher than a keynote speaker.

The pitch of his voice and the dramatic pattern of his sentences had people clapping and nodding in agreement. From his perch next to President Lincoln, Maximilian could even hear a shouted "Hallelujah!" on more than one occasion.

The feeling of the crowd seemed to take on a different **temperament**—that of the inspirational Dr. Martin Luther King Jr.

Maximilian was entranced.

> *"And so even though we face the difficulties of today and tomorrow, I still have a dream.*
>
> *It is a dream deeply rooted in the American dream."*

The words rang through the **humble** mouse's ears. The notion of a *dream* that all Americans—white and black, male or female, rich or poor, human or animal—could share made Maximilian's chest swell. He hung on every word Dr. King spoke.

It was a much different speech than the one Lincoln had given in Gettysburg. King was much more confident than Lincoln. In many ways the messages being delivered were the same. But, the way Dr. King spoke was full of **poise**.

Maximilian turned to see Marian's reaction to the speech. She sat quietly, her eyes closed, with her small gray paws cupped in her lap. Leonard, Judith Anne, Earl, and Elaine watched closely, taking in each word that left Dr. King's mouth.

> *"I have a dream that one day this nation will rise up and live out the true meaning of its* **creed***:*
> *'We hold these truths to be self-evident, that all men are created equal.'"*

It was what Oliver had taught him in Boston on the first day of his journey. Hadn't the colonists wanted everyone to be equal?

It was what Robert Franklin had wanted when he took his family across the great plains of America. He hoped to be able to provide for his family and to earn a decent, fair wage.

It was what those traveling down the currents of the mighty Mississippi River and those daring the trip across the Atlantic Ocean

to reach the banks of Ellis Island had all wanted —to be free.

Maximilian felt proud as he listened to these words. He felt proud on this summer day in 1963 because it was what he too had hoped to achieve through his quest. He wanted to live in the glen that his ancestors had helped build. He wanted to feel safe and secure in a home he loved with so many other animals.

> *"I have a dream that my four little children will one day live in a nation where they will not be judged by the color of their skin but by the content of their character."*

It is pure poetry, Maximilian thought, *both in how it was written and how it was delivered.* He shared the crowd's appreciation of King's majestic speech. He had not disappointed.

As Maximilian looked to Marian one last time, he noticed a single tear rolling down her soft cheek. King delivered the last few verses of his speech:

"Free at last! Free at last!
Thank God Almighty, we are free at
last!"

Chapter 11:
A NEW SOUVENIR

As quickly as the crowds had gathered in the Memorial Plaza, they left. They took with them the wisdom and inspiration of those that had spoken to them that summer day.

"Are you sure you cannot stay for dinner, Mr. Maximilian?" Marian asked one last time.

"No, really," Maximilian insisted with a smile, "I need to be on my way." He shook paws with Leonard and Earl. He sent a friendly nod to Judith Anne and Elaine.

"I'm sorry to hear that, dear," Marian said sadly. "I certainly appreciate the company you've given this old, blind mole."

Maximilian missed his home and his mother. But this last twenty-four hours with

Marian had helped. He leaned toward Marian and gave her a soft kiss on her cheek.

Despite her ability to detect things around her, this surprised her. She smiled at him.

"Do you know, by chance, what your name means, Maximilian?" Marian asked.

He thought for a moment. It had always struck him, and others, as being a unique name. But, he had never asked about its origin.

"No," he responded. "I can't say that I do."

Marian took his paw and whispered to him, "It is Latin for *greatest*."

Maximilian felt his face warm as she squeezed his paw.

"Someone must have thought pretty highly of you to give you such an honorable name, don't you think?" she asked.

Maximilian nodded.

"Remember, my friend, that one does not always see using one's eyes," Marian said. "By the way," she said with a suspicious curl of her brow, "you never did tell me what you had there, behind the monument."

Maximilian looked at the other moles, but said nothing. Marian smiled at him.

Taking Leonard's arm, she and the others slowly made their way past the second column. They turned to the right and out into the darkness that had fallen over Washington.

Maximilian had only a few hours to wait until the time machine was ready again. Sitting with his back to Lincoln's statue, Maximilian thought very seriously about what Marian had said to him. Cradling his pocket watch in his paw, he watched the minute hand climb past the twelve—one more hour.

The memorial was quiet again, like when he had first arrived the day before. Suddenly Maximilian heard footsteps echoing off the hard marble floor in the clear night air.

Maximilian's pulse quickened. He willed himself to go see who this unexpected visitor was. Chances were they were just another tourist or someone cleaning up after the day's events, but Maximilian wished to take no chances.

He pressed his back flat against the stone pedestal and carefully made his way around the side and toward the front. The light in the Lincoln Monument shone bright as Maximilian peered out from the shadows.

Maximilian could not believe his eyes. He had never expected to see Dr. Martin Luther King Jr.

Maximilian held his breath and watched. The man who had delivered the most passionate speech he had ever heard bowed his head and began to pray.

Maximilian watched and thought, *What is he saying? Is he asking for advice? For strength?*

Part of Maximilian wished to say something to the reverend. He wanted to tell him how proud the president would have been. Maximilian knew Lincoln's dream of a unified country was the same that Dr. King wanted for the nation. But he didn't say anything.

Finally, Dr. King placed his hands in his pockets and gazed toward Lincoln. Alone in the chamber, he looked humble. Then, he turned, adjusted his suit coat, and walked into the night.

As he did, Maximilian heard a noise. It was the faint sound of something hard, possibly metal, hitting the marble slab. The gleam of an object caught Maximilian's eye. Without thinking, he raced out into the open to see what it was.

Maximilian found himself in Lincoln's shadow looking at a fine, gold cuff link with the letters *MKL* engraved on it. It must have fallen from King's shirt sleeve when he removed his hand from his pocket.

Maximilian ran to the mouth of the monument with the cuff link under his arm. Peering out onto the empty mall, Maximilian searched, but Dr. King was nowhere to be seen. A few random wrappers and papers scrolled along the ground in the otherwise still night.

Maximilian breathed in the warm summer air. He analyzed the cuff link. The letters were a beautiful cursive script, and the rim was gold. Maximilian wondered who had given the reverend these special accessories. When would he realize that one was missing?

Maximilian sat next to one of the columns until his watch chimed the top of the hour. He hoped that Dr. King would return to get his missing cuff link—but he didn't.

The moon shone bright in the late August sky. The stars sparkled brilliantly like diamonds. If Maximilian had not known any better, he could imagine himself in a different time. He could have been with Madeline on the open prairie of Kansas or Nebraska. Or he was in Ashling's company on the deck of a slow Irish immigrant ship making its way toward New York Harbor. And, if he allowed his mind and imagination to truly drift, he could imagine these very stars dotting the late night sky in Tanner's Glen.

It had become clear to Maximilian that he was alone. Dr. King would not be returning to look for his missing cuff link. It was time for him to test the time machine yet again. Another chapter in his journey was coming to an end.

Maximilian carried the cuff link back to the time machine. He took a moment to look one final time in the direction of President Lincoln. Maximilian said nothing, but he looked at the statue, much like Dr. King had.

Returning to the time machine, Maximilian began preparing for the trip that would hopefully take him home.

Chapter 12:
LEARN TO SEE

The time machine was charged and ready for Maximilian to set the coordinates. It was so quiet in the monument that he thought about taking a few minutes to write in his journal. After all, when you had a time machine, what were a few more minutes in the grand scheme of things?

Opening the hatch, Maximilian was confronted with another problem. The time machine was full. Finding room for himself might prove to be a challenge. Maximilian began to rearrange his things as creatively as he could.

He had managed to discard most of what he had originally brought with him. He had made space for Lincoln's button and his gold nugget. Maximilian also found a safe place for the torn page with Mark Twain's quote and the four-leaf clover from Ashling at Ellis Island. Between these cherished **souvenirs** and his wool coat, space was limited.

Maximilian decided that he could manage if he were to sit on his coat and rest his hind paws on the cuff link. The idea of leaving it behind had crossed his mind, but only for a second. He liked that these things linked him to the people he had met and the events he had witnessed.

The cuff link fit perfectly at the base of his chair. It would be crowded, but Maximilian had no problem making the adjustment. He breathed on the shiny cuff link and polished it with the sleeve of his shirt.

Maximilian removed his journal from the time machine. He opened it and realized that he had only two blank pages left. He also managed to locate his pencil, worn from use. He did not, however, need much lead for the entry he planned on making this night in Washington.

Maximilian turned to the second to last

page, wet the tip of the pencil on his tongue, and wrote:

August 28, 1963—Washington, DC
One dream can impact many. Learn to "see" the true value of an animal without using your eyes.

With that dedication to Dr. King and Marian, Maximilian packed the last of his things, climbed inside the time machine, and closed the portal door behind him.

Chapter 13:
A FAMILIAR PLACE

The familiar coordinates were set. It was quiet in the time machine. Maximilian fastened his seat belt. His paw brushed the four-leaf clover he had carefully folded next to his seat.

The dashboard lights sprang to life. Maximilian drew a deep breath and began the starting sequence. The familiar spinning began.

Maximilian squeezed his eyes shut. The spinning got faster. The **centrifugal** forces that Maximilian had learned to endure began to overwhelm him. Beads of sweat burst from his forehead and the heat within the time machine became unbearable.

What was happening? Was the time machine too full? Was there a weight limit?

Maximilian gripped the armrests until his small joints ached. Just when he thought he could not bear any more, the time machine began to slow. Maximilian strained to get a breath. As soon as he could, he undid his seat belt and relaxed.

The date he had set remained lit on the panel in front of him. Maximilian knew by now that this did not mean anything. He could hope though.

Maximilian rummaged in his pockets for his handkerchief, but it was nowhere to be found. Unrolling his shirtsleeve and sliding his paw inside, Maximilian unhooked the portal latch. Cool steam rolled inside. Maximilian climbed outside and collapsed on soft, sweet hay.

He lay flat on his back, exhausted. The smell of hay was familiar. It triggered a series of memories from his childhood. He ran strands of it through his fingers and sat up with it sticking to his sweaty back.

Maximilian rested with his tail draped out in front of him, dirty and stained like the rest of him. Suddenly, he sat up perfectly straight. His heart quickened and he jumped to his feet. In front of him was an old, wooden slotted door. Maximilian ran to it and peered out.

The sun had just risen above the horizon. Fresh dew glistened on blades of beautiful green grass. Maximilian looked around **frantically**.

He knew this place! He breathed the air in and felt the ground beneath his toes.

Of course he knew this place!

Maximilian was in Farmer Tanner's old barn!

Chapter 14:
HOME

Maximilian fell to his knees. He began to laugh as tears ran down his face. For the first time in a long time, the tears were ones of happiness.

He could not believe his eyes. Maximilian had been inside Farmer Tanner's barn so many times. It was dark inside, but the loft and the old farming equipment were all the same.

Maximilian got to his feet and looked out through the wooden door again. He had to reassure himself he was back on the farm and not dreaming.

Farmer Tanner's house stood directly in front of him. It was not his imagination. The white house, built in the mid-1800s, sat on lush, beautiful farmland. Its white-painted exterior was chipped and in desperate need of a fresh coat of whitewash. Yet, to Maximilian, it was the most beautiful house he had ever seen. He shook his head in disbelief.

Suddenly, a thought dawned on Maximilian. Even though he was now in the correct place, he still had to find out if he was in the correct year.

The barn had been unused for several years. A newer, bigger tractor had been far too large for this barn. Farmer Tanner had built a more expensive one on the property.

Maximilian wondered if this had led to his economic problems and to the loss of the entire farm to the bank. Regardless, Maximilian felt as though the time machine would be safe for now.

He dusted himself off and closed the door to the cockpit. Then, he slid on his stomach under the worn barn door. The dew felt cool on his stomach as the early morning sunshine struck his face.

As Maximilian exited the barn, he saw the woodland trees for the very first time. Somewhere in the depths of the forest were his home and his mother and sister.

As close as he had come to completing his quest, he still had a job ahead of him. He continued to stare at the fence row that divided farmland from forest. Suddenly, it dawned on Maximilian that he had thought very little about how he would save the farm once he arrived.

The cool air swept over Maximilian's fur. Straightening his back and legs, Maximilian began a slow jog toward Farmer Tanner's house.

He had arrived back in the glen . . . but what day was it?

Chapter 15:
FINALLY!

Maximilian's paws slipped only once or twice as he waded through the moist grass toward the farmhouse. It was early and Maximilian expected Roman W. Rooster to make his morning announcement at any moment.

Roman was an older rooster, but he was known throughout the county for his brilliant red beard and loud *cock-a-doodle-doo*. The routine of the farm and the regular everyday schedule of the animals was something that Maximilian had missed when he was away.

The three-story house loomed in front of Maximilian. The wrought iron weather vane in the shape of a fish pointed west. It felt so good to be home.

Maximilian reached the side of the house and the trellis that Mrs. Tanner used to drape her morning glories. He carefully climbed to the windowsill and peered in the dining room.

It was early, but Farmer Tanner had already started his work day. Mrs. Tanner was busy in the kitchen frying bacon and brewing coffee. Maximilian noticed that there was a small tear in the window screen. He squeezed through, careful not to catch his clothes or his tail.

The Tanner dining room was simple, but tasteful. The table and matching chairs, the corner cabinet, and the sideboard were all oak and of great pride for the family. The table was strewn with papers and pieces of mail. A calculator, writing tablet, and pair of reading glasses sat idly by on a pile of documents.

Maximilian studied the room. It was neat and organized, but it was quiet inside the farmhouse. Maximilian felt heavy with sadness. Mrs. Tanner tended to her duties in the kitchen but did not whistle, hum, or even listen to the radio. Aside from the clattering of an occasional pot or pan, it was completely quiet at 324 Tanner's Lane.

Maximilian used a nearby lamp cord to slowly make his way to the floor. He scampered to a chair leg to climb onto the paper-covered table. The whistle of the coffeepot was followed shortly by Roman's famous call signaling the beginning of yet another day on the farm. Maximilian began to study the documents laid out before him.

An opened envelope on the top of the pile caught his attention first. Actually it was the stamp of a certain president that made him chuckle.

"You certainly are everywhere, aren't you?" Maximilian whispered. He leaned close to the sticker of President Abraham Lincoln.

Bacon hissed in the frying pan behind him. Maximilian licked his lips as his mouth began to water. Remaining on task, he used both paws to draw the folded record from its envelope and spread it out before him. Holding his breath, Maximilian began to read.

It was a statement from the bank and it was dated for October 11, 2013.

Maximilian smiled again and sat on his back legs. An overwhelming sense of relief took hold of his entire body. If the letter was received yesterday by Farmer Tanner and if it had been dated the day before, when it had been shipped, then today, in fact, was . . .

October 13, 2013.

Chapter 16:
THE BAD NEWS

Maximilian had managed to arrive safely in Tanner's Glen on his desired date. What still remained a mystery to him was how, exactly, he was going to save his home and the farm from being lost to foreclosure.

The letter from the bank was short and to the point. Running a paw over the text, Maximilian began to read. The statement informed Farmer Tanner that he was behind on his taxes—over $5,000.

Maximilian shook his head. He was feeling less than confident that he could help Farmer Tanner keep the farm. Based on the notes scribbled on the writing pad and the math that had been worked out, Farmer Tanner had come to the same conclusion.

The other papers on the table were a combination of charts, tables, and tax returns.

Maximilian licked his pointer finger and began sorting through the pile. He saw a steady decline in wheat production, a steep downturn in milk prices, and late tax payments by Farmer Tanner. Any one of these things would have been difficult for the farm, Maximilian knew. But all of them working together were just too much to overcome.

Maximilian stood and stretched, his mind swirling around the facts. The situation was certainly bleak.

Mrs. Tanner had finished preparing breakfast. She was now cleaning dishes while staring blankly into the lukewarm dishwater. Maximilian noticed that her eyes were dark and sunken from lack of sleep and that her hair was uncombed. He felt for her. It was up to him to save the farm for both the Tanners and his own family. He certainly did not endure all that he had to reach this point and fail.

Maximilian made his way to the hardwood floor. The boards were polished and shone brightly despite their age. Grooves were revealed in several of the floorboards, the result of years and years of chairs sliding in and out from the table.

He decided to take a tour of the house. He felt safe with Farmer Tanner tending to his morning chores and Mrs. Tanner occupied in the kitchen.

The other rooms were just as simple as the dining room. They all had the same thoughtfulness and attention. The sitting room had a love seat. A rocking chair sat next to an old stone fireplace. The mantel held twigs of a willow tree in a canning jar and several framed pictures that had begun to yellow over time.

Maximilian began to understand the silence and the overwhelming sense of gloom in the Tanner home. The same sense of hopelessness had overcome him as soon as he read the final notice from the bank. Five thousand dollars was a lot of money, certainly more than Maximilian had ever seen before.

Chapter 17:
AHA!

Maximilian looked at the pictures surrounding the hearth. Some of the images were in color. Some of them were black and white, but they all showed family and friends in much happier times.

Could the people in these pictures help the Tanners? Did they know that Farmer Tanner was about to lose the farm?

Everything Maximilian saw in the house reminded him of home. The rush he had felt earlier that morning when he had first arrived was gone.

A noisy engine in the driveway signaled the return of Farmer Tanner for a quick breakfast. Mrs. Tanner let the screen door slam behind her as she went to greet him. Maximilian listened closely, but neither of them spoke a word. They both came back into the house looking more defeated and discouraged than ever.

Farmer Tanner was a tall, thin man. His denim overalls were almost identical to Maximilian's Cajun bullfrog friend Bogart's. The difference was, Farmer Tanner's hung loosely on his slight frame. He laid his work gloves on the radiator near the front door and ran a hand through his thinning hair.

Farmer Tanner walked quietly to the dining room table. He stacked the collection of paperwork and sat down. Mrs. Tanner brought him a mug of coffee with a small glass of creamer. She served him a plate of eggs and bacon.

The screen to the front door had a small slit in it. Maximilian made his way through the screen door and onto the front porch. He removed his vest and unbuttoned his collar. Closing his eyes, Maximilian could see all the papers he had just examined on the table. The numbers were so big and the gap between money owed and income seemed impossible.

Maximilian looked out over the farm from beneath the hanging porch swing. It still seemed unreal to Maximilian that he was back home. This was the only home Maximilian had ever known and now it might all be lost.

He had thought about it at every stage of his trip. Now, Maximilian felt like he was hearing about the bank's foreclosure for the very first time.

Slowly, Maximilian forced himself to catch his breath. He buttoned his shirt again as he looked out over the neglected waterwheel. The image of the Abraham Lincoln postage stamp jumped into his head.

He paused.

Five thousand dollars . . .

Maximilian's eyes went wide. His heart pounded. He raced to the end of the porch and looked at the outbuilding that now housed the time machine.

"Of course," he said to himself. "Of course!"

The time machine held the answer to this problem. Jumping to the soft grass below,

Maximilian began running toward the barn and the time machine.

The wind blew through his fur as he ran. He felt as good as he ever had before. He knew the answer. Maximilian knew how to get the $5,000!

Chapter 18:
AN IDEA FORMS

The sunshine splintered through the side panels of the old barn. A single ray of golden light fell directly on the time machine. It was resting where Maximilian had left it that morning.

Maximilian shook his head.

Why had it not dawned on him earlier? The answer to his problem had been in the time machine this entire time!

Maximilian broke the seal to the hatch and leaned in. He began reaching for all of the items he had collected throughout his trip. He laid them carefully on the soft hay in front of him. Then, he stepped back to admire his work. Each item represented a memory, a stitch in time, and a leg in his journey. They had each helped bring him to this very spot here today.

There was the navy blue button with the presidential crest. He had found it on the floor in Gettysburg moments after Abraham Lincoln had left. Next, Maximilian looked over the finely polished gold nugget he had pulled from the crystal clear waters in Silver Springs, Utah. The mere thought of Madeline made him blush. The piece of gold was small, but certainly large enough to carry some value.

Maximilian used the nugget of gold as a weight to hold down his next treasure, a carefully creased piece of paper. It was not so much the paper itself that held any value, but the writing on it:

> *Twenty years from now you will be more disappointed by the things that you didn't do than by the ones you did do. So...*
>
> *Explore.*
> *Dream.*
> *Discover.*
>
>   *Samuel Clemens*

Maximilian could picture himself sitting in the rafters of a fine Mississippi riverboat with Bogart. The writer, dressed in his white suit, sat on the outskirts of the dance floor. *Surely this autograph carried some value,* Maximilian thought.

Finally, his eyes fell on his latest keepsake, the finely polished cuff link of one Dr. Martin Luther King Jr. This souvenir alone might fetch the $5,000 Farmer Tanner needed to ward off the bank's foreclosure.

The time machine had been a constant frustration for him. But, the "mistakes" made by the device would ultimately save his home. Without the failed attempts to reach Tanner's Glen, he would not have had any hope of raising the funds needed to save the farm.

Maximilian stood for a long time admiring his collection. He gathered together the button, the gold nugget, the scrap of paper, and the cuff link. Maximilian began thinking of how he could get them all into the Tanner house. More importantly, how he could pass along his plan to the man who needed the money.

Chapter 19:
WAITING FOR NIGHTFALL

It was still early in the day, but Maximilian did not want to go far. Nathaniel had warned him not to come into contact with any animal, including himself, when he arrived at his desired time in history.

Maximilian intended on taking no chances. He would remain in the barn until darkness fell over the farm. Then, he would execute his plan.

He would need to get the valuables from his trip into the Tanner house. He would also need to write some sort of letter explaining his intentions. He wanted to be an **anonymous** donor, a friend of the family who wished to remain unnamed.

Farmer Tanner could sell the items and raise the money he needed to repay the bank. He might even have some money left over to make other improvements to the farm.

"Don't get too far ahead of yourself, Maximilian," he said out loud. He still had a lot of work to do. Maximilian had managed to avoid many dangers throughout the past weeks. He did not want to make a mistake now.

The warm autumn sun climbed higher in the sky. Maximilian began writing the note he would pen to Farmer Tanner in his head. Maximilian needed the wording to be perfect. He did not want to leave any detail out.

He read his journal for inspiration and to help with the specific wording. When he entered the Tanner dining room again, he needed to be fast.

The sounds outside the barn began to fade as the sun set. Soon, another day on the farm wound to an end. Maximilian sat with his back to the time machine and closed his eyes. It had been an exciting day—a day filled with renewed hope. It had also been a busy day and Maximilian was tired.

As the stars began to poke through the sky and the moon slowly revealed itself, Maximilian fell asleep . . .

Chapter 20:
IT'S TIME

The darkness was so deep that Maximilian had a difficult time determining where he was exactly. The moon was completely blanketed by storm clouds. Large raindrops began to pelt the ground and the large maple leaf Maximilian huddled beneath. The storm had overtaken the glen with very little warning.

Maximilian's shelter threatened to surrender to the winds and to the downpour. He watched in horror and disbelief as the trees around him parted. The sound of rolling thunder gave way to the sound of heavy motors making their way through the brush.

Maximilian knew what was coming. He had seen it before, in a dream. The ground would start to heave under the might of the bulldozers. Maximilian braced himself. Then, to Maximilian's disbelief, as quickly as it had all started, the storm stopped and the engines died.

What was happening? He'd had this dream before and it had never played out like this.

Maximilian remained under the torn, weathered leaf and shook, waiting for what would happen next. He convinced himself not to wake up, to see the dream to the end.

In the fence row, where the machines had been before, Maximilian saw something. He squinted and tried to make out exactly what it was. Standing there, amongst the thistles and thorns, was the **silhouette** of a mouse.

Maximilian stopped shaking and came out from the leaf. The clouds were parting, but Maximilian still could not make out the mouse's identity. It was a stranger, yet someone Maximilian had met before. Something about this mouse made him feel safe.

Maximilian tried to call out, but he could not. The words would not come. He stared at this mouse as his face gradually came into focus.

Maximilian blinked hard. The mouse was brown and had a kind face. His whiskers were white and he wore a dress shirt and vest, similar to Maximilian's. Then, he noticed something else—a silver pocket watch.

The mouse did not say anything. He simply stared at Maximilian. Unable to speak, Maximilian tried to move. He tried desperately to go to him, but he could not. Maximilian was helpless.

The mouse reached inside his pocket and brought out his watch. Flipping it open and then closed, the mouse gazed at Maximilian and smiled. Then, he mouthed something before retreating into the cover of the glen's underbrush.

Maximilian slowly opened his eyes. He was drenched in sweat, his cheeks sore from crying. Part of him wanted to shut his eyes again and pick up the dream where he had left off, but it was no use.

In the fleeting time he had to send a message, the mouse had chosen four, simple words. Four words that Maximilian repeated to himself, alone in the darkness, in the old barn on Tanner's farm.

"It's time, my son."

Chapter 21:
MISSION ACCOMPLISHED

Maximilian gathered the four items of value onto his coat. Then, he carefully laid the sleeves over top of them, tying them together in a pouch. Lifting it slightly off the soft earth, he gauged its weight. It was less than a pound and easy for Maximilian to carry from the barn to the farmhouse.

Having dozed for several hours, Maximilian still had a few hours left before daybreak. He could make it there and back before Farmer Tanner would rise to start his day.

Maximilian placed his full weight against the rickety barn door. He managed to open it just enough for him and his coat of treasures to slip out.

The temperature had dropped considerably. Maximilian shivered slightly. His breath **wafted** from his mouth and disappeared somewhere above his head.

Maximilian took a deep breath of cool night air and trudged across the front lawn. He followed the same path he had that morning. The moon provided just enough glow to light his way.

Maximilian replayed his dream over and over as he went. He was amazed at how real it had all seemed. The nightmares he'd had since beginning his trip had all shown the destruction of Tanner's Glen. Not only had those images changed, but the message had been delivered by his father, who had disappeared when he was only a year old.

The Tanner home grew bigger as Maximilian drew closer to the front porch. The screen door, as well as the front door, were both closed, but neither were locked. Maximilian managed to squeeze his way inside.

The Tanner house was completely silent

except for the ticking of the parlor clock hanging in the next room.

Breathing heavily, Maximilian headed to the dining room. Standing at the table leg, Maximilian placed his coat on the floor.

Feeling the energy drained from his body, Maximilian decided to carry each item separately up the table leg and safely onto its surface. He started with the button, then the

gold nugget, followed by the scrap of paper, and finally the cuff link. Maximilian's watch chimed four o'clock.

The four tokens from his trip lay in front of him, each one representing a different point in history. In the dark, Maximilian located a clean piece of paper and broke the lead tip from a freshly-sharpened pencil. Wiping sweat from his brow, he began to write.

The words came to him with ease, like they had when he had written in his journal. The pencil lead scrolled effortlessly across the paper, Maximilian's tongue tucked between his lips in concentration. He took only one break to allow his aching paw to rest.

> *I trust that these historic artifacts will allow you to free yourself from debt. Please accept them, use them, and rebuild the farm for all those who call it home.*

Maximilian sat on the table, alone in the dark, and rested. There was no more worrying about his mother and his sister. No more worrying about how he would save the farm once he reached Tanner's Glen.

It had all worked out in the end. Now, there was only one thing left for Maximilian to do . . . go home.

Chapter 22:
TIME TO GO HOME

Maximilian made his way through the tall, swooping sweet grass as the early morning sun hit the horizon. He fought the urge that he'd had since arriving. He wanted to rush into the woods to see his mother and sister. He wanted to go home. The old oak tree might as well have been a million miles away.

Maximilian reached the barn and walked inside. If Farmer Tanner followed his instructions, the farm would be saved. Taking comfort in this, Maximilian removed his coat, folded it, and placed it in the time machine.

Maximilian followed the cedar beams as they crisscrossed through the eaves of the barn. He had never noticed them before. Now, he thought, he might never see them again. He very well might spend the rest of his life jumping from one wrinkle in time to the next.

Maximilian climbed inside the time machine one more time. It felt different somehow. Maximilian was more nervous than each of the other trips combined. He was so close to being done with all of this.

Could Nathaniel's time machine possibly get it right two times in a row?

It was time to find out.

Maximilian fastened his seat belt. He tightened the buckles and flipped on the power switch. Breathing a sigh of relief, he was happy that there was enough power for one more destination. For the first time, Maximilian set the coordinates for a new date and time—two weeks into the future. He needed to return to the precise time he had left Nathaniel's workshop.

With everything finalized, Maximilian took a moment to study his one remaining souvenir —Ashling's four-leaf clover. It was simple, but it gave him strength.

Reaching for the start button, Maximilian hesitated. Right then, his pocket watch chimed. It was exactly twenty-four hours since Maximilian had arrived back in Tanner's Glen.

It's time, Maximilian thought. *It's time.*

He pressed the button, held his breath, and prepared himself for disappointment.

Chapter 23:
ANOTHER TRY

The time machine surged and then came to a rest. Maximilian sat without moving, without undoing his seat belt. He sat quietly in the dimness and listened.

Nothing.

He began to guess where he was this time. Maybe he was in a different country . . . Maybe he was back at a location he had already been.

Maximilian sat some more before unlatching the straps. He reached for the door lock, when he heard a rustling from outside the time machine.

Maximilian froze and fear swept through his body.

The rustling continued as Maximilian strained to see out the small window. Craning in a rather uncomfortable position, Maximilian watched as a large tail passed in front of his face. It startled him at first, until he realized exactly what it was he had seen.

"Maximilian?" the voice from outside the time machine called. "Maximilian!" the voice echoed again with renewed enthusiasm.

Maximilian closed his eyes. He was completely exhausted, but he was back in Nathaniel's workroom.

A cool, crisp breeze blew through the lazy willow trees. This breeze marked the change in seasons. It swept away the longer, carefree summer days. Now the autumn months for winter preparation were blowing into Tanner's Glen.

A small field mouse sat perched on an old ash log in the middle of the glen. He gazed about in wonder and thought of this change of seasons.

A strong gust chilled the small mouse and he pulled his **waistcoat** tight. Just then, the familiar chime of his pocket watch sang out.

He carefully removed the watch from his breast pocket and opened it.

It was six o'clock. The mouse thought about his family and wondered what they were doing at that moment. He knew his mother would be preparing supper. She would worry if he were any later.

Maximilian jumped to the ground and disappeared into the woods.

About the
Civil Rights Movement

The March on Washington on August 28, 1963, was the largest civil rights demonstration in US history. An estimated 250,000 people representing many ethnicities and backgrounds listened to speeches that day.

Included among the activists that spoke that day was the young preacher Dr. Martin Luther King Jr. He was one of the leaders of the civil rights movement.

One hundred years after Abraham Lincoln's Emancipation Proclamation, Dr. King stood with the Lincoln Memorial as his backdrop. Dr. King and his supporters asked the nation's leaders for racial equality.

In his now famous "I Have a Dream Speech," King called on Washington to help minorities everywhere recognize their dream of life without restraints and a country without discrimination.

The impact of the march and of Martin Luther King Jr.'s speech were felt over the following years. That was when the Civil Rights Act and the Voting Rights Act of 1965 were passed. Both were important laws that President John F. Kennedy had introduced and fought for before his death in 1963.

Glossary

acquaintance - someone you have met briefly.

activist - a person who practices direct action in support of or in opposition to an issue that causes disagreement.

anonymous - not named or known.

architect - a person who plans and designs something.

boycott - to refuse to deal with a person, a store, or an organization until it agrees to certain conditions.

burrow - a hole or tunnel dug in the ground by a small animal for shelter.

centrifugal - an apparent force tending to pull a thing outward when it is rotating around a center.

charismatic - having a special magnetic charm or appeal.

contraption - a gadget or tool.

creed - a set of beliefs.

critic - a person who finds fault with something.

democracy - a governmental system in which the people vote on how to run their country.

eerie - strange or creepy.

frantically - marked by fast, nervous, or worried activity.

generation - a group that is living at the same time and is about the same age.

hearth - the floor of a fireplace.

heirloom - something of special value handed down from one generation to another.

humble - not proud or arrogant.

humidity - the amount of moisture in the air.

immigrant - a person who enters another country to live.

impolite - not showing good manners by the way you act or speak.

impose - to force into the company of or on the attention of another.

intimidating - able to fill with fear.

minority - a racial, religious, or political group that differs from a larger group in a population.

momentum - a moving object's speed or force that is caused by its weight and motion.

obelisk - a four-sided pillar that tapers at the top like a pyramid.

observation - the act of seeing or sensing with careful attention.

pedestal - a base that something sits on.

podium - a stand to hold a book or script at a height easy for a person to read to a crowd.

poise - a way of carrying oneself that is calm and pleasant.

prejudice - hatred of a particular group based on factors such as race or religion.

Reconstruction - the period after the American Civil War from 1865 to 1877. During this time, the Southern states were restored to the Union.

riveted - to have one's attention caught and held completely.

rural - relating to the country or farmland.

silhouette - the outline of a figure or profile.

souvenir - something you keep to remind you of a person, place, or event.

temperament - the attitude that affects how one behaves.

transcontinental - crossing a continent.

unique - being the only one of its kind.

waft - to move or go lightly on the wind.

waistcoat - a vest.

About the Author

Maximilian P. Mouse, Time Traveler was created by Philip M. Horender. Horender resides in upstate New York with his wife, Erin, and their dog, MoJo.

Horender earned his Bachelor of Arts in History with a minor in education from St. Lawrence University. He later obtained his Masters in Science in Education from the University at Albany, the State University of New York.

He currently teaches high school history, coaches swimming, and advises his school's history club. When he is not writing, Horender enjoys biking, kayaking, and hiking with Erin and MoJo.